P9-CED-426

For Dad, an astute forester,
and Mom, an elegant correspondent.
Thank you for inspiring me! — C.B.M.

For Ania and Maciek
What's meant to be will always find its way — K.N.

STERLING CHILDREN'S BOOKS
New York

An Imprint of Sterling Publishing Co., Inc.
1166 Avenue of the Americas
New York, NY 10036

STERLING CHILDREN'S BOOKS and the distinctive Sterling Children's Books logo
are registered trademarks of Sterling Publishing Co., Inc.

Text © 2019 Cathy Ballou Mealey
Illustrations © 2019 Kasia Nowowiejska

All rights reserved. No part of this publication may be reproduced, stored in a retrieval system,
or transmitted in any form or by any means (including electronic, mechanical, photocopying,
recording, or otherwise) without prior written permission from the publisher.

ISBN 978-1-4549-2120-2

Distributed in Canada by Sterling Publishing Co., Inc.
C/o Canadian Manda Group, 664 Annette Street
Toronto, Ontario M6S 2C8, Canada
Distributed in the United Kingdom by GMC Distribution Services
Castle Place, 166 High Street, Lewes, East Sussex BN7 1XU, England
Distributed in Australia by NewSouth Books
University of New South Wales, Sydney, NSW 2052, Australia

For information about custom editions, special sales, and premium and corporate purchases,
please contact Sterling Special Sales at 800-805-5489 or specialsales@sterlingpublishing.com.

Manufactured in China

Lot #:
2 4 6 8 10 9 7 5 3 1
01/19

sterlingpublishing.com

Design by Ryan Thomann

The artwork for this book
was prepared digitally.

WHEN A TREE GROWS

by **CATHY BALLOU MEALEY**

illustrated by **KASIA NOWOWIEJSKA**

STERLING CHILDREN'S BOOKS
New York

WHEN A TREE GROWS IN THE FOREST,

two things could happen.

It becomes a scratching post for Moose's itchy antlers, and the tree sways gently side to side.

OR...

CRASH-BOOM!

Moose pushes a little too hard, the tree falls on a cave, and the bear inside wakes up.

When a bear in a cave wakes up, two things could happen.

He rolls over and falls back to sleep.

GRR-ROAR!

Bear stomps outside.

When Bear stomps outside,
two things could happen.

Bright sun! He squints and
stumbles back into the cave.

BUMP-THUMP!

He plows into Moose and
sends Moose stumbling into the road.

When Moose stumbles into the road,
two things could happen.

He gets safely to the other side.

SCREECH-THUD!

A truck swerves around Moose
and lands in a ditch.

When a truck lands in a ditch, two things could happen.

Squirrel pelts the truck with acorns until it drives away.

YIPPEE-YUMMY!

It's a Nifty Nuts truck! Squirrel leaps on board.

When Squirrel leaps on board, only **one** thing can happen.

VROOM-VROOM!

Squirrel is off to the big city.

When Squirrel is off to the big city,
two things could happen.

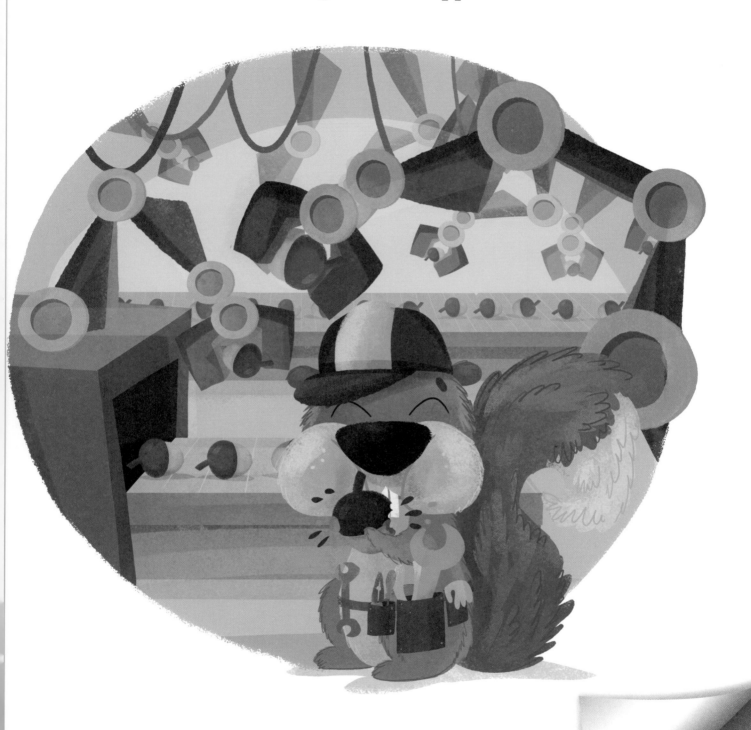

He gets a job at Nifty Nuts
as a quality control inspector.

SLAM-
CLICK!

He is alone,
with no place to go.

CLOSED

When Squirrel is alone with no place to go, two things could happen.

He is discovered by a talent scout, and becomes a star of stage and screen.

OR...

SNUFFLE-SNIFF!

He feels homesick.

VISIT STATE PARK

When Squirrel feels homesick,
two things could happen.

He starts saving money for a bus ticket.

OR...

SCRIBBLE-SCRATCH!

He writes a letter to Moose.

When Moose gets a letter,
two things could happen.

He doesn't know what it is,
so he eats it.

ZOOM-ZOOM!
He races to the city to bring Squirrel home.

When Moose brings Squirrel home,
only **one** thing can happen.

HOORAY-HOORAY!

Moose and Bear throw a Welcome Home party
with an all-you-can-eat acorn bar.

When Squirrel celebrates at an all-you-can-eat acorn bar, two things could happen.

Squirrel eats every last acorn.

MUNCH-SCOOP-PLOP!
Squirrel eats just the biggest acorn.

Then he plants the rest,
and they grow into a forest . . .